The Case of the Disappearing Seals

Written by Barbara Moore

Illustrated by David Cox

sundance
A Haights Cross Communications Company

Published by
Sundance Publishing
P.O. Box 740
One Beeman Road
Northborough, MA 01532-0740
1-800-343-8204

Copyright © text Barbara Moore
Copyright © illustrations David Cox

First published 2002 by
Pearson Education Australia Pty. Limited
95 Coventry Street
South Melbourne 3205 Australia
Exclusive United States Distribution: Sundance Publishing

Guided Reading Level J
Guided reading levels assigned by Sundance Publishing using the text characteristics
described by Fountas & Pinnell in their book *Guided Reading*, published by Heinemann.

ISBN 0-7608-5814-4

3rd

Contents

Characters

Jessica loves to spend vacations with her grandfather on his island.

Leo is Jessica's younger brother. He is usually hungry.

Lily is Jessica's friend. She is interested in studying animals and plants.

Chapter One

The Island

At last, summer vacation had arrived. Jessica and Leo, her brother, were off to stay with their grandfather for two whole weeks.

Grandfather lived on an island close to the coast. He was a marine biologist. He studied the plants and animals on the island.

The kids were very excited. Jessica asked Lily, a friend from school, to come with them.

Jessica and Leo's parents drove them to the town nearest to the island. Then they all caught the ferry across to the island.

Grandfather was waiting for them on the porch of his home.

"Welcome, welcome!" he said. "It's so good to have all of you here. I'm happy to meet you, Lily. Sometimes it gets a bit lonely on the island. Now I'll have someone to cook for besides Max."

Max was a brown-and-white dog with big, moist eyes. He barked and jumped on and off the porch excitedly, wagging his tail so hard that it almost fell off.

Jessica's parents left to catch the next ferry back home. "Have a great time," they called as everyone waved good-bye. "We'll see you in two weeks."

"Well, let me show you to your rooms. Then I'll make us some dinner," said Grandfather, who loved to cook.

Chapter Two

The Seals

Grandfather cooked a delicious dinner of spareribs, corn on the cob, and crispy french fries. Then Jessica, Leo, and Lily helped him wash the dishes.

Grandfather told them about his early life on the island. His own father had taken him for long walks along the cliffs.

Grandfather loved taking photos of the different plants and animals. He wrote detailed notes about them in his journals. He had studied science at college so that he could be a marine biologist. He told them about all of the animals that lived in and near the sea.

Grandfather told the kids about a
colony of seals. He said they lived on the
rocks by the sea, not far from his house.

"Would you like to go to see them
tomorrow?" asked Grandfather.

"I'd love to see the seals!" exclaimed
Jessica.

"Oh yes," agreed Lily and Leo.

"You know, I'm worried about something," said Grandfather. "Every week, I walk to the cliff to check on the seals. When I first started doing this, there were lots of seals. I put tags on many of them in the colony. That way I could track them. But now only half of the colony is left."

"Only half?" said Jessica.

"Yes. They seem to be slowly disappearing, and I have no idea what is happening to them. If only I had time to look into it. But I have to get another project done first," said Grandfather sadly. "Anyway, it's time for bed. Sleep well, and we'll go to see the seals tomorrow."

Jessica stayed awake for a while. She was too excited to sleep. She kept thinking of everything Grandfather had said. She wondered if maybe she could help. Finally she went to sleep. In her dreams she saw shiny seals swimming far away from the beach and her grandfather calling to them.

Chapter Three

The Mystery

The next day, after a delicious breakfast, Grandfather took them to see his favorite places on the island. He put a picnic lunch in the backpack. There were sandwiches, cake, and a thermos full of hot chocolate. Max came, too.

"Soon you will be able to see the sea," said Grandfather. He walked briskly. The kids had trouble keeping up with him. "Come on, kids!" he laughed.

Finally they reached a flat, grassy area. Jessica stopped in amazement. They were at the top of a high cliff overlooking the open sea.

"This is where I'm doing my plant project," Grandfather explained.

"This is a great place!" Lily said.

"You can see for miles around," said Grandfather.

Leo moved closer to the edge of the steep cliff. He wanted to look over the side.

"Careful, Leo. Don't stand too close to the edge," said Grandfather. They all obeyed and stood a little farther back, staring at the stunning view.

Grandfather was excited, too. He
explained to them that the line where the
sky meets the sea is called the horizon. The
sky curved above them like a giant blue
dome. It was a beautiful day with only a
few puffy white clouds.

Then Grandfather said, "Let me show
you some of the animals."

At first Jessica, Lily, and Leo found it
difficult to see the animals because they
blended in so well with their surroundings.
Grandfather showed them how to use the
binoculars to see things close up. They each
took a turn.

Grandfather pointed out the different varieties of birds. There were seagulls and terns everywhere.

Lily also found some seagull nests and saw a chick in one of them. She gave the binoculars to Jessica and Leo so they could see the chick.

Then Jessica, Lily, and Leo watched
the seals playing in the water. Some were
flipping over and gliding into the sea.
Other seals sat on the rocks sunbathing.
They were very noisy, barking and calling
loudly. The kids watched excitedly.

"Grandfather, can we go closer to have a better look?" asked Jessica.

"Yes, follow me. There's another place farther down."

Now Jessica could see what the seals really looked like. Their shape, graceful beauty, and playfulness astonished her.

The seals were not afraid of Jessica, Lily, and Leo. They did not mind them being there at all.

That night Jessica had trouble sleeping again. She was haunted by the mystery of the disappearing seals. Was someone taking the seals away? Maybe there were some sharks in the area.

Just as she was falling asleep, Jessica had an idea. Maybe she, Lily, and Leo could solve the problem. Grandfather had said he didn't have time to find out what was happening. If they watched the seals for a while, they might find the answer. She couldn't wait to tell the others about her plan.

Chapter Four

The Plan

Jessica woke up early. Lily and Leo were still sleepy when Jessica told them about her plan.

"Let's try to find the missing seals while we're here," Jessica said.

"What a good idea," said Lily.

"What's a good idea?" said Leo, rubbing his eyes.

"We're going to find out why the seals are missing," explained Jessica.

"Can I come, too?" asked Leo sleepily.

"Of course you can. We can work together to find out what has happened to the seals," said Jessica.

Grandfather cooked them eggs and hash browns for breakfast. "I'm studying the plants on the cliff top near the seal colony," he said. "I need to spend the next week in that area."

Jessica grinned at the others.

"Can we go with you and use the binoculars, please?" asked Jessica.

"Of course," said Grandfather.

"I've packed some sandwiches, cookies, and lemonade so we won't be hungry. Are you ready for action, Max?" asked Grandfather.

Max led the way along the path to the place where Grandfather was working. Jessica, Lily, and Leo could watch the seals from there. They each took turns looking through the binoculars. They could clearly see the seals with the brightly colored tags on their flippers.

Jessica suggested that they try to count the seals each morning and note the time when they saw them. She wanted to make an estimate of how many seals there were in the colony. She was hoping to figure out how quickly they were disappearing.

Each morning, the kids watched the seals. Jessica wrote down the details in her special notebook. Lily and Leo helped her count all of the seals they could see. In the afternoons, they went exploring.

"Be careful," Grandfather told them all. "Stay on the paths and away from the cliffs."

Chapter Five

The Solution

Each day, Jessica, Lily, and Leo would study what Jessica wrote in her notebook. But they couldn't tell anything from the results. The number of seals they counted was different each day. After a few days, Jessica noticed only a small decline in the number of seals. She was disappointed.

That afternoon when they were
exploring, Lily pointed down a path that
was overgrown with grass. "Why don't we
go down there? It heads to the other side
of the island where we haven't been yet,"
Lily said to the others.

"Good idea," said Jessica, hoping that
something new would cheer her up.

"How far is it to the other side?" asked Leo as he pushed through some branches. They had been walking for over an hour.

"I don't know. Let's go just a little farther," said Jessica.

"Okay," said Leo. "But can we have something to eat first? I'm hungry!"

Jessica and Lily laughed. They ate some granola bars and apples.

"Follow me," said Jessica after they finished their snack. They walked in single file along the narrow path. Soon they could see the sea in front of them.

"Listen. What's that noise?" asked Jessica, looking around.

"What noise?" asked Leo.

"I can hear something, like barking. It doesn't sound too far away," said Jessica.

They followed the direction of the odd sound. Jessica was holding the binoculars and walking toward the noise quickly.

"Don't get too close to the edge of the cliff," warned Lily. "Remember what your grandfather said."

Jessica looked around and saw a path that went over to the side of the cliff. The others followed her.

Suddenly, as they came around a large rock, they could see the cause of the barking noise. Seals!

"Wow," said Jessica. "Look at all of them!"

"Far out," said Lily.

"Cool," said Leo, amazed by the sight.

Jessica studied the seals closely. They were the same species as the ones near Grandfather's house. Then she couldn't believe her eyes. The seals had colorful tags on their flippers! These were the missing seals. They must have set up a new colony, thought Jessica.

Jessica was very excited. She could hardly wait to tell Grandfather.

From a distance, Grandfather could hear the kids shouting his name. Max went out to meet them as they came running across the grassy area.

Jessica yelled excitedly, "Grandfather, we know what has happened to the missing seals!" She then told him about the seals they had found.

Grandfather smiled proudly at them. "One day you'll all make fine marine biologists!" he said.

"I'd like to be a biologist," said Jessica. "But we found the seals by accident. It wasn't very scientific."

"You know part of being a good biologist is the willingness to explore," explained Grandfather.

"If that's true," said Leo, "can we go explore the kitchen? I'm hungry!"

They all laughed as they headed back to Grandfather's house.